ENCOUNTERS IN THE WOODS

VOLUME 8

ETHAN HAYES

CONTENTS

ONE

CHASED BY BIGFOOT

IT'S BEEN four weeks since my disturbing encounter with what I know was a Sasquatch or Bigfoot. What makes this story all the worse was I didn't even want to go on this hiking trip. My friend, Chaney, had been begging me to go hiking at the state park, but I had heard some stories from friends about weird occurrences and to be honest. I'm just not the biggest hiker or camper. In fact I don't like the outdoors all that much, now I can say I officially hate it.

Anyway, after being persistent, I relented. We set the date for the next weekend and planned the trip.

Chaney was a good friend and had all the gear we'd need, minus the hiking boots which I agreed to go buy.

Well the day came and we set out early. We were going to make it a fun and easy day. The overall hike would be five miles, but the trail was easy, mostly flat and he promised to stop numerous times so I would be able to rest. All he told me was the hike would be 'fun'. I'm one for fun, but hiking wouldn't ever make that list of fun things.

We set out and not a quarter mile in, Chaney stopped, took off his pack, unzipped it, reached it and came out with two beers. My eyes widened and a laughed.

He said he promised this would be a fun hike and what makes a hike fun was having a beer as you went. This was my kinda of hike.

I happily took the beer and we proceeded on. We laughed and joked and one beer turned to another and another. After the third beer, we had made it to the turn around, but I wanted to relax a bit and take in the view. We set up on a bench which overlooked a long field with tall grasses. Chaney pulled two more beers from what seemed like a bottomless pack and handed it to me.

Our conversation turned from jokes to a serious tone when we got talking about my ex. At the time I was a bit sad after a breakup, (looking back now, I'm so happy that relationship is over), and Chaney admitted this was why he insisted on having me go hiking. He could tell I was depressed and thought the fresh air, coupled with some beers with a friend would help.

I agreed, it had helped and I was really enjoying the day.

We ate some lunch, finished a fifth beer and was annoy to head back. I can say I recall being a bit tipsy, but who cared. We had the rest of the day to make it two plus miles. It was fine. We slung our packs on and I stepped off, but before I reached the trail, Chaney called me over, his voice sounded excited.

He told me to look out in the field about a hundred or so yards to the north east, he said he saw something big moving. He lifted his hand and using his index finger pointed.

I looked in the direction but didn't see a thing and told him so.

He promised me it was there.

I joked and said that maybe he'd had enough beers and that I was cutting him off.

I went to turn around when out of the corner of my eye I spotted movement, I looked carefully and saw the thing he'd seen. It was dark, and appeared to be covered in fur or hair. It didn't seem that tall, but I saw what clearly looked like a head and shoulders, then it stood.

What I thought was short was nothing close to being accurate. The grasses were at least two to three feet tall and this thing towered another four feet over it, making it at least seven feet tall.

I instantly got scared and told Chaney that we should head back.

He didn't want to. He took off his pack and began to dig for his phone. He said he was going to get a picture. As he did this, I again stressed that we should leave.

Just as he found his phone, I looked up and saw the thing was coming towards us and fast. I cried out that it was coming our way.

Chaney looked up, his eyes widened and he stuttered that we needed to go and NOW.

He stuffed the phone back in his pocket, slung his pack over one shoulder and took off for the trail. I was right behind him. Before I entered the woods I looked over my shoulder to see the thing was closing in and FAST!

We sprinted through the woods, my focus on the trail beneath me as I had almost tripped twice over protruding roots. Chaney who was in better shape than me was a good twenty yards or more in front and moving away.

What's the joke, when you're being chased by something, all you need to do is be faster than the other guy, well, I was the other guy. As I huffed and puffed and my chest burned, I swore that if I survived this I'd get my fat ass into shape. Nothing was worse than needing your body to do something and it just wasn't physically up to the task.

My entire body felt weak and my head swooned. I felt sick to my stomach and my skin was tingling, no doubt from the lack of oxygen. And to add insult to injury my muscles were cramping.

I looked up and Chaney was now not anywhere in sight. I was really scared now as I heard branches cracking behind me, this thing was in the woods and chasing me, I would have said us, but like I mentioned, Chaney was long gone. And you know what, I deserved it. How had I let myself get so out of shape.

The five beers weren't helping either, I could hear the beers swooshing in my stomach, with frothy burps coming up every few seconds.

The trail made a sharp turn, it was a way point I remembered and it told me I was more than half way. I finally hit a root and went face first into the trail. My chin split open and I could feel the warm blood flowing down. I didn't bother to look, I scrambled to my feet, but before I could take another step, my stomach had other plans. I projectile vomited my sandwich, chips and what felt like a gallon of beer onto the trail, and my boots.

Behind me I could hear the thing crashing through the woods, its footfalls sounding heavy, like loud thumping.

I didn't even bother to wipe my chin or face and carried on.

Ahead of me I heard someone hollering. It was Chaney, he had made it back to the car. My heart sang out a joyful chorus. I was close and soon I'd be safe and sound.

My relief was quickly dashed as a large rock came crashing down on the trail just in front of me. I leapt over it and looked back to see the thing not twenty yards away. It was HUGE, it stood in between two large oaks and had its arms in the air in a menacing pose. It was black, like a similar color of a black bear. It 's shoulders were broad and its arms were long, at least that what they appeared to be. It's face wasn't completely covered in hair as I could see what looked like grayish skin. It had a thick brow, large wide eyes that were sunken in, a wide flat nose and its mouth was wide with thin lips.

My heart sank, this was a monster right out of a nightmare and it was close. I began to wonder if I was going to die. I faced back towards the trail and continued on, I heard more crashing behind me. I could have sworn it was now on my heels.

Ahead of me I heard Chaney hollering for me to

hurry, but I was at my limit. My chest burned, blow was flowing down my shirt from my split open chin and my muscles were tapped. I was giving all I had and I can say now that I wasn't giving up, but this thing was about to catch me and there wasn't a thing I could do.

Just as I felt all hope was lost, I saw Chaney waving. I could see the light of the trail head, I was close to the parking lot and hopefully to surviving (I know this sounds dramatic, as it's obvious I survived, but that's how I felt then). I again tripped and fell, this time my knee got busted up, I got to my feet and started to hop. It was then I noticed I didn't hear any crashing behind me. It took all the discipline I had not to look back, I was close to getting out of the woods and I wasn't going to stop until I did.

I called out to Chaney to come help me and he did. With my arm draped over his shoulder, he assisted me out of woods and to his car where I again vomited and laid on the ground out of breath.

I administered first aid to my chin and knee where I had lost a chunk of skin as I begged for us to leave. Over and over I told him I'd seen it, I'd seen a monster. He told me he saw it too, but further away.

After cleaning me up, we loaded up and headed home. We talked the entire drive home and I asked if he wanted to stay over, he did. We spent that night going over what we'd both seen and took to the internet to find out more information. Of course we found a lot.

I never told anyone else about it until I again had curiosity if there had been other sightings in that park. I found out that others had over the years, but none reported being chased.

I think that the thing didn't want to hurt us because if it had wanted to it could have. It could have caught my fat ass and there wasn't a thing I could have done about it. I think all it wanted to do was scare me and well it accomplished that.

Two things resulted from the crazy hiking trip, I never went hiking again, but I got myself into amazing shape; we're talking six pack abs and a lean body. I would never allow myself to be so out of shape that it almost cost my life. Yes, I know it didn't want to kill me, but what if it had, I would be here detailing this story to you. I lived and I plan on living a full life.

TWO

THE UNSIGHTLY THING

THE STORY I'm about to tell happened a few years ago. I wrote it down not long after it happened and have since gone back to get it as detailed as possible. I wanted to ensure my encounter flowed and had a presence all its own. So here goes:

————

The large and picturesque landscape of Ketchikan, Alaska was the home to my two bedroom flat bungalow where I usually came to, to unwind and escape the life I had in busy New Jersey. It was basically my second home and I wished I could live there all the time.

My time training in the army when I was in my twenties down into my thirties had prepared me somehow for this wild cabin living I so loved to immerse myself in whenever I could. I worked as a builder in New Jersey and so building this cabin in the woods with ample land around it was pretty interesting work. It was definitely not easy being out here alone by myself and working tirelessly into the night for seven months straight but it was fun.

The cabin was complete with the stunning porch facing the dense trees in front of the building and the silent stream that ran a little way ahead. The wide porch with the wooden railing wrapped around it was my favorite place in the entire cabin. It was just too efficient for a place of any kind of relaxation, grilling meat over an old open grill I called Jessie and even shooting.

Man, I loved to shoot. I had a couple of moose heads hanging around my house at the top of furnaces, elk skins also displayed here and there and one black bear rug smack dab in the middle of my living room. It was never a chore getting to do these things and what came after them.

After my wife had left me and took away my kids

with her, my cabin was all I got and I hoped that one day, I would die here.

That wish almost came true a little sooner than I expected.

Yes, my cabin was a beauty in the middle of nowhere in the woods; a picturesque habitat for a quiet and reserved man like me.

This was what I always thought until the ninth of June snuck in like a thief in the night.

That was exactly what I thought when I woke up with a start on that fateful night. I was sweaty and breathing heavily like I had just chased a deer through the woods hoping to kill it.

But I had not had a nightmare. I did not know what had woken me up until I heard them again.

The deep guttural grunt and the snapping of branches from a deep part of the woods right outside my bedroom window.

I did not waste any time. I got up to my feet and quickly reached for my gun underneath my bed.

It was here again.

Earlier that day, I was rounding up a catch I had in the stream; I was busy gutting out the bunch of fish I had caught that evening when I heard a sounds.

To me, it seemed like a big animal was walking through the dense forest and parting the trees as it went.

I could feel my heart beating a little heavier than it normally did. I heard things like these all the time. It was either they were big bears just trudging past my cabin or tall moose just wanting to sneak a peak of the hunter who had killed two of their kind.

But this one...This was different. I did not know what came over me. I dropped everything I was holding and rushed to a shed that housed all my tools in front of my cabin and hid in it. I pressed myself against the wall of the small and dark building and I could hear it. My heart, beating so loudly and quickly. I thought I would die.

I have served in the army and fought against terrorists. I have lived out here in these woods through the day and night and I have killed animals so much that I knew the sounds they made by heart. But this one terrified me.

It sounded like a good mix between a bear and...a man.

I did not know what to call it. The guttural groans and the powerful breaking of branches sent fear to my heart and I just knew I had to hide.

Who knew what it was?

I heard it again.

It was right outside the shed and close to the running stream where I had been fishing for the past hour. A howl suddenly shook the forest and gasped. Then, I heard munching sounds and another growl.

Was whatever was out there eating my catch?

I had to see what it was. I spotted a window at the other side of the shed and moved to it, trying not to make a sound. I got to the window and with sweat dripping down my forehead and unto my shirt and my mouth wide open trying to get more breath in and out so I don't faint from curiosity and fear, I looked out.

There it was.

It was large and tall. It had hair or was it fur all over its muscular body. Its head was as large as the boulders that sat in the stream, so big I wondered if I really was looking at a real, moving and sound making thing. It was completely black in color and altogether resembled an ape standing on its two legs. It bent down to the pile of fish guts that I had left there in fear and grabbed a handful. Standing back to its full height, I watched the beast shove the meat down its throat.

Behind me, I had no control over it and I could not remember just how it happened but a shovel fell.

And it made such a loud sound that I thought I would shout at.

I looked back to the beast from the shovel on the ground and saw that it now faced the shed I was hiding it.

This time, I could no longer breathe. I was about to shout when I heard a mighty roar from the ape and then its thundering footsteps on the ground, through the water and into the trees.

Just like that, it had disappeared.

Until the night came...

After I had grabbed my gun from beneath the bed, I ran to the window in just my boxer shorts and searched the pitch black night for the creature I had seen earlier that morning.

I knew it was a Bigfoot.

I always knew they existed no matter what anyone said. Seeing one earlier that day had put the fear in me of them.

Now, I had a chance to catch one.

I readied my shooting gun, aiming it outside the window and looked out, searching the black night for a moving creature that resembled the one I saw that afternoon.

I saw nothing. I continued to search with my one opened eye, ready to shoot when suddenly, the moon cleared and a part of the woods showed the silhouette of the hairy beast bending to grab unto a boulder, a short distance from my cabin. I aimed again and was about to shoot at the animal when I realized what it was trying to do.

And how many there was behind it.

My eyes opened wide and I duck for cover just as a large boulder flew through the air and right at my window where I was about to shoot at the creature, at them.

I rolled to the corner of the house and watched the boulder fall right into the unlit fireplace. I wanted to go back and try to shoot at the creatures but common sense told me to stay where I was. Soon, the sounds of angry growling, howling and grunting filled the forest where my cabin home stood. I felt surrounded and I thought I was going to die that night.

I felt another rock hit the house and I knew she was going to go down. If I let it.

There was another rock with a loud roar after it crashed through another window and another and another and another, trying to break the house down.

I had to do something or no one would know where I was or how I had died.

Without thinking, I rolled over the floor right in front of the broken window and blindly aimed outside. I praised Mary for having the common sense to always load my gun to the brim before sleeping, a little behavior I got from the army that helped me that night.

I began to shoot wildly. I heard a deep scream and roars all around me and they seemed to get closer.

But I did not stop shooting.

They got closer...

But I spun around and shot at the other window through which one of the creatures' rocks had broken into.

Before I could decide on what my fate could be because my gun had almost run out of bullets, I heard a loud cry and right after, the stomping of feet.

They ran farther and farther away from me.

I did not realize I had stopped breathing since I woke up and I stayed in the same position with one knee on the ground and my hands holding tightly to my gun which was aimed at the large hole in my window until the night was back to its silence.

Not a sound was heard again for the rest of the night.

I could remember getting up from that position when I heard the faint sounds of birds early the next morning. I got up, packed a few things and left the cabin with my gun.

Today marks a year since I returned to the cabin. I never told a soul what had happened until now. Thank you for allowing me to get my story out.

THREE

HAIRY MAN

MY ENCOUNTER HAPPENED BACK in 1997 when I went out on a four wheeler with my ten year old nephew. We were in some backwoods in Washington State and the area we were in was private property. We weren't legally supposed to be there but I had been going to this one particular area of land for years at that point and it was a really awesome place to not only ride four wheelers but also to just hang out. I had even gone to some parties there when I was still in high school. At the time of the encounter I was around twenty five years old and had never gotten caught being in this area and didn't even know who owned the land at the time. I have come to find out, since the incident I'm writing about here and everything that followed it, that the land is government owned and there isn't much more information than that about it anywhere, including online. I believe the government in this area is hiding something and that there's a reason this land is littered with no trespassing signs and warnings. I also believe that's why there is hardly any information about this particular area of land online still to this day. I believe that's because of what my nephew and I saw when we were trespassing there, on our four wheeler, way back in the late nineties. I still can't understand one hundred percent what it was and my nephew only has a vague memory of it so he is no help. I have been obsessed with figuring this out ever since that day but honestly have come no further with understanding exactly what it is we saw out there. At least, I'll say I can't prove or back up what I THINK is happening not only out there but all over the world. It heavily involves alleged Bigfoot sightings, too. Let me start at the beginning.

There were several hundred acres of extremely dense forest located a fifteen minute walk from my house at the time where I still lived with my parents. That was the house I grew up in and so the whole place was very familiar to me. I remember purposely not telling my sister that I was taking her son to private land where I could have gotten in trouble if we were caught. I didn't even know what the consequences would even have been. During all of the parties I had attended on that property in my high school career we always made a ton of noise and we never got caught or in trouble for any of it. We never came across another human being and nothing weird or sinister had ever happened to any of us, as far as I knew at least, while we were out there. I had gone there alone dozens of times and in fact that was one of my favorite things to do now that I was an adult loner who barely had any friends now that high school had been over for almost eight years and everyone I knew either moved away and started their own family or moved away to go to school or just didn't have time for me anymore because I was single and not a good fit for their married lives. That's another situation though and I'll try to just stick to the facts about that day and what I believe I saw out there. My nephew and I rode the ATV, with me driving and him sitting on the back. He had never been on one before and that's why, also, I wanted him to have a really great time and a place where he could just explore some.

We got there and I had him go under the chain fence, walk right by even more no trespassing signs and lift the chain for me to drive under. I drove the ATV very slowly with him following next to me until we came to a very wide stream. I rode over it with him on the back and then just took off. We rode like this for about ten minutes and then I let him have his turn being the driver. I was hanging back and taking pictures of it for his dad. His dad hadn't been able to go with us that day because he was working and my nephew didn't want to wait. His father promised him that if he learned to ride one the right way- safely and properly- he could have one of his own for his upcoming birthday. It was a big deal for him at the time because he was only ten. We ended up being out there way longer than expected and before I knew it an hour had passed. My nephew was having so much fun and I didn't want to end it yet so I agreed we could spend some more time riding around. I took a ton of pictures and eventually, about two hours after we had first crossed the large stream, we had circled back to it and I decided it was time to leave. He was ready to go at that point too and all in all it had been a great day. I had three photos left on my disposable camera and I told him to ride through the stream one more time so I could take the last three pictures. He did as I asked and as I raised the camera to my face and looked through the lens, I saw something step out from behind some trees in front of and to the right of my nephew. It was about eight feet tall and walked on two legs like a human. It was covered in black hair and at first it didn't seem to notice us, despite not only the noise of the ATV but also all of the noise we were just making in general. I snapped one picture but it was of the thing walking past him. Suddenly my nephew yelled for me to look.

I moved the camera from in front of my face and saw my nephew struggling to stop the ATV. If he had kept going he would have gone right into this thing and he knew enough to not want to get any closer to it than he already was. The creature turned around just as my nephew yelled for me and started pointing at it. The four wheeler stopped but my nephew was so shocked and nervous he fell off into the water. All of a sudden, as I ran toward him to help him, the creature also started walking briskly toward the both of us. I wanted to get him up and out of the water so we could turn around and run. I planned on either hiding for long enough that the creature was nowhere in sight and retrieving the ATV or, at that point, I was even considering just running away and returning later on for the vehicle. The latter turned out to be what had happened. I ran towards my nephew who was struggling to get his bearings while this gigantic creature briskly made its way toward him at the same time. In my effort to help my nephew I dropped the camera and it went downstream. I got him up just in time and we both turned to run and get the hell out of there. The creature let out a very loud growl and picked the ATV up, effortlessly, and threw it at us. Luckily we were already far enough away that it didn't come close to us at all. I looked back only once and it was only to see the ATV landing on its side and the creature turning and running away from us and towards a nearby tree. We booked it out of there and I took my nephew home. I left him at the front door of my parents house and immediately went back to investigate what I had just seen. I was so annoyed with myself for losing the camera but didn't want to take the time to stop and get another one. I figured there was no shot in hell of me seeing something like that again anyway but I was wrong.

I was back in the exact same spot within a half hour and I immediately found my ATV still lying in the same spot where it had landed after being thrown. I grabbed it and pushed it off to the side. I was going to lie in wait for a little while and see if I could catch a glimpse of that thing again. I had no idea about Bigfoot or anything like that back then but I was determined to figure out what it was we had seen. I thought there would surely be some sort of simple explanation for it. I had no idea how complicated the explanation was though, not back then. Within minutes I heard leaves snapping in front of me and I peeked out from behind the tree. I saw the same entity walking across the stream in almost the exact same spot I had seen it the first time. It looked over and it must have noticed the four wheeler was gone because it stopped and started to advance on me, without knowing it, because it was trying to see where the ATV had gone. I didn't know what I was thinking or why I did what I did next but I stepped out from behind the tree and allowed it to see me. It growled a very loud and thunderous growl but now I was close enough to see it more clearly. It had human eyes, nose and mouth but the rest of its face was covered in black hair. The hair on the face was much shorter than the hair on the body. I looked it dead in the eyes but thought for sure I was going to have to once again run for my life. I was sure that it was going to attack me but instead something very strange happened. It looked like it was scared. It flinched when it saw me and despite the growl there was something about the eyes that reminded me of a scared child. A human child, mind you, not a scared animal.

Suddenly it turned and ran from me. It didn't run extremely slow or at any type of superhuman speed but just like a regular human being ran. It then did something else that was weird when it tried to hide its gigantic and very dark body behind some trees while I stood there and watched it do so. It's like it didn't comprehend that I was watching it or that I would see it doing that. It then peeked from behind the trees and saw me still staring at it. It then ran off into the woods. I had a decision to make about whether to go after it or not and at that moment I decided I had seen enough for one day. I rode the ATV back out of the woods and to my parent's house. My nephew hadn't mentioned what we had seen to anyone and really didn't say much about it to me. One of the few things he did say to me though is something that changed the course of my life forever. He told me that the thing looked like the "cavemen" he had learned about in school, only with more hair. That's when my research started. We both got cleaned up and when my sister and nephew left that night I went to the library and started my research. This was right before the internet was really anything at all and the library and regular books were all I had. I spent hours every day researching and it became an obsession. I found out that there used to be human beings who lived beside us, back in "the caveman days" and the only difference between them and us was that they were covered in hair. The male and females were covered in long, shaggy hair.

They lived off the land right beside us but when the areas of land where we all made our homes began to become populated but scttlers, we- the non hairy humans- decided to try and blend in and live among them while our hairy friends stayed behind and remained living in the shadows off of the land. I know how crazy this sounds but if you look it up, it's all real information.

I have gone back to that area of land and came across either the same creature or one just like it more than two dozen times since that first day I accidentally stumbled across that one. I leave little gifts of fresh fruits, vegetables and fish and while I can't say I've made friends with them, I do know that when they see me coming, they know I'll have food. They don't run and hide from me anymore except, of course, when I have any tech with me to document what I am seeing and doing. There have been a few people who have been able to get photographic and video evidence of these other humans left over from a time period long ago forgotten by us- when we were also hunters and gatherers and that's how we lived our lives. Do you want to know something? I don't believe in Bigfoot either and I wholeheartedly and fully believe that Bigfoot is another variation of the feral human being that I had come to know and love so much.

Recent issues with my health along with more security being put on that land has made the last ten years or so impossible for me to get back to them and spend more time. I know what I saw and I know what I know. I believe Bigfoot is what I saw. Only Bigfoot isn't Bigfoot, it's a type of neanderthal man left over from long ago.

FOUR

VERY STRANGE CREATURE

I GREW up in the wilds of Kentucky in the United States. Three-fourths of the land I lived on was woods and I spent most of my time growing up inside of them. There was always the feeling of being intensely watched but other than that I can't think of a single time I felt or saw anything strange. That is, until the day of the encounter I am writing about now. I will never forget what I saw nor will I ever be able to forget the terror that I felt as this thing, whatever it was, stared at me as though burning a hole through my soul. I have five siblings and my encounter took place back in the early 1970s. I was the youngest and so most of the time I was left to my own devices. I used to have so many adventures in the woods surrounding my house and it never got boring for me either. The woods surrounding my house and all along my property were dense and had streams running through them in more than one spot. My father and brothers and I would go fishing together but at the time of this encounter I hadn't been hunting with them yet. There were vague legends of Bigfoot and myths about hairy, feral men who would kidnap you and turn you feral but I took all of them with a grain of salt and at face value. Until the afternoon when I saw the creature.

I used to love pitching my small tent in the backyard and hanging out all night under the stars. I would have a little food and some drinks, a flashlight and some comic books. That was enough for me. I loved falling asleep to the cacophony of sounds the wildlife at night made. It's all very different now and I've always regretted that my kids and grandchildren never got the chance to experience the great outdoors the way that I used to when I was their age. By the time I grew up, moved out and started a family of my own, my parents had sold the property and moved to a rental home that was much smaller and easier for them to manage and maintain.

Once they retired they didn't want to have to do anything as far as upkeep a whole property and several dozen acres. I didn't blame them but it was disappointing nonetheless. I was about fifteen or sixteen years old and I had done something to get myself in trouble in school. My parents grounded me but I managed to have the punishment not include my being able to camp outside. My father gave in rather quickly and so I set up my camp and he helped me build a little fire. It was late in the afternoon and just getting dark. I said goodnight to my parents and siblings and settled in for a night of fresh air and comic book reading. If anything were to happen, or so I reasoned with myself back then, then it would be at night. It's not really that I was scared or anything but I did sometimes get a little spooked when I had to get up and go to the bathroom. That's where I think the encounter started. I had to go to the bathroom in the middle of the night.

I walked into the woods just a little bit. I had my flashlight on and right when I was done going pee I thought I saw something move in the periphery of my vision. I quickly spun around in that direction and shone my flashlight on the spot where I thought something had just been. Whatever it was, at least from out of the corner of my eye, looked like it was running. However, once my light reached that spot, I didn't see anything. I stood there silently for another minute or two, shining my flashlight all around to make sure that it wasn't a bear or something else that could possibly smell my urine and/or attack me while I was asleep or something. I didn't see anything and after another minute or two I turned and went back to my tent. I woke up several more times that night because I thought I heard someone or something creeping around my tent. Everytime I looked there would be nothing there. I wasn't a superstitious or religious kid by any stretch of the imagination and I certainly didn't believe in anything supernatural or paranormal. I was thinking whatever it was was more along the lines of some regular animal that wanted to eat the little bit of food I had taken out there with me for the night. There was something about the way the walking sounded though that didn't quite sit right with me. It sounded like it was on two legs, whatever it was, and I couldn't think of a single animal that walked that way. There was no reason for another human to be out there and even my siblings wouldn't have been foolish enough to come out there and try to scare or prank me. That's just not the type of things we did and not the sort of relationship that we had. However, by the end of the night I thought that that was exactly what was happening. I tried my best to ignore it and after three more times of being woken up to hearing these strange creeping sounds, I decided it was my siblings and I wasn't going to give them the satisfaction of seeing me scared or hunting for them. I was definitely rationalizing but didn't know that at the time. I went back to sleep.

I was still angry that I had been grounded for what I believed was such a small infraction. I don't know what it was that I had done but I remember thinking to myself that it was no big deal. When I woke up in the morning I went inside and had some breakfast. I cleaned up my things from outside and then decided to take a walk through the woods. There was one very large stream that I liked to visit and sometimes I would even fish there. I grabbed my fishing rod and tackle box, changed my clothes and took off into the woods to spend the day fishing. I left my parents a note because they were still asleep when I went inside to eat and change. It took me about fifteen minutes of slow walking to get to the stream I was looking for. I knew right where it was but the paths that led there were all precarious and tricky so I had to take my time. I was a safe and careful kid, it was just my nature. I made it to the spot and got everything set up. I was sitting there for about an hour and I had caught about three small fish when I decided to get up and stretch my legs out a bit. I was starting to get hungry and was thinking about heading back home soon. That's when I heard what sounded like someone walking up behind me. The sound was like something walking on two legs and it sounded like whoever it was was purposely trying not to be heard. I stood perfectly still and tried to listen without letting whoever it was know that I had heard them. Again there was no way it was actually a human being unless it was someone in my family coming to try and scare me. That didn't make any sense but it was once again the only thing that I could think of at the time. The walking noises stopped just as suddenly as they had started and after another minute or two of standing there intently listening, I decided to pack everything up and go home.

At that point it was more than just hearing something and I was really starting to get scared. This was the same type of sound that I had heard all around my camp the night before. I still had a fairly long way back to go if someone or something were out there intending to do me harm and so I figured I better start walking. As I bent down to pick up my tackle box and the fish that I had just caught, I heard a splash in the water. I knew as soon as I picked my head up I would finally come face to face with who or whatever had been stalking me since I had been sleeping in my tent the night before. I took a deep breath and looked up. Standing about twenty feet away from me, in the middle of the large stream, there stood some type of creature. I will describe it to you now the best that I can. The water went up to its knees but it still looked like it stood at around nine feet tall. It had a small head for its massive body and it was about seven inches wide in the chest area. The nose was similar to that of a pig's nose and the mouth looked almost nonexistent. I could see two thin lines where the mouth should have been but it literally looked like someone had merely done a half assed job of drawing the mouth on with a thin pencil. It was so creepy. All of the hairs on my body stood up and a chill ran through me. I just stared at it and it stared back at me.

This creature wasn't only ridiculously tall but it was also extremely thin. It was eight feet tall or more and it looked like it only weighed about one hundred and ten pounds, if that much. It wasn't hairy and seemed to be naked although I couldn't make out any sort of genitalia or anything that would give away its gender either. Its skin looked like it was super tightly stretched against its bones and body. It was all very unnatural looking. The creature and I just stared at each other for a moment and then the most terrifying thing of all happened. It looked at my hand that had the fish I had caught in it and then back at me. Suddenly it opened that teeny tiny little pencil thin mouth and it looked like it was stretched out in a perfect circle shape. It was huge now and the jaw looked like it was dislocating, almost like a snake does when it is devouring its prey. A sound came from the terrifying and seemingly toothless mouth. It was a sickly pale color, almost with a greenish tint to it. The sound that came out sounded like the shriek of a banshee- or at least what I had always imagined that would sound like. The water and earth below me and the trees all around me started to vibrate. Suddenly my head felt like it was under so much pressure it might explode. I dropped everything and keeled over in pain. I covered my ears and closed my eyes but that didn't seem to help. I got out of there as fast as I could. I was stumbling and half blind for the first minute or two. As soon as I was out of the creature's sight, the sound stopped and everything returned to normal again. All I heard was one more splash and a growl and then the woods were back to sounding and feeling normal again. I, however, would never be the same.

I made my way back home and when I got there I realized I had a nose bleed. I needed to immediately go and lie down. When my mother saw me she was immediately worried and I told her I wasn't feeling well. I had an extremely high fever on and off for the next week and a half. I couldn't leave my bed or keep much food down. My mom wanted to take me to the doctor but I kept putting her off. I was having non stop hallucinations and fever dreams of the creature from the woods. I often wonder if it was actually in my room at night while I thought I was only dreaming of it. I have a strange feeling it was there but there's no way to prove or really know it. While I did go back in the woods many times after I had this encounter I was always much more careful and I never went fishing again. I believe that the first night it had wandered onto my campground in the backyard and smelled either me or my food. Then, I believe it recognized my scent, probably from all of the times I had urinated in the woods, the next day. I believe then it was after the fish and the reason it came to the stream in the first palace was probably to fish. It saw I already had fish in my hand and figured it was an easy meal. I wonder what would have happened had I not had the fish already. Would it have come after me? I truly have no idea and haven't found any more information about anyone else having any encounters like this one or really anything about it on the internet at all. What I saw defies logic and wasn't any kind of animal or cryptid I had ever heard about or that I have even come across up until now. I don't know anything else and am just glad I never ran across that thing or anything else like it ever again.

One other thing I often think about is why it was only that night and the next afternoon that this thing seemed to be tracking me. What was different about that piece of time than all of the others I had spent in those woods, fishing and camping in my backyard? I wonder if anyone out there will recognize the creature I described and if I will finally get some more information, if not some very much needed actual answers.

FIVE

LIZARD PERSON IN JOSHUA TREE

MY FAMILY and I have always gone on camping trips and at some point we just started visiting all of the national parks in the country. We did this year after year as I was growing up and we always had a good time. It would be me, my parents and both of my younger brothers. While we had always visited one well known camping spot or another ever since I can remember, we started going out of our way to all the parks when I was about six years old. It was like a new adventure for our family and a great way for us to spend some time together. The year that I was seventeen my parents decided that they wanted to visit Joshua Tree National Park in California. We had visited there once or twice before because when there was somewhere we really liked, we would go a few more times. This is just to give you all some background so please bear with me. That year for one reason or another I couldn't or didn't want to go with them. I'm pretty sure that vacation fell on the same week as when I had been invited to go somewhere else with my then girlfriend and her family. Being a teenager, my girlfriend won out. My parents agreed to let me skip out and they went to Joshua Tree alone with my brothers. However, something really strange happened in that it was the first year they ever came back without staying a full week or ten days. They were gone for four days and then called me to tell me that they had decided to leave early. I was really confused but my father said they would tell me more about why they had left once I got home from my trip with my girlfriend. That didn't happen though because when I got home it was like no one wanted to talk about why they had left so quickly when the other times we had all gone there we had loved it so much. My parents just said that my mom wasn't feeling well and my brothers never said anything else. I never thought to press them or prod for more information and just assumed they were being weird. Maybe my mom had gotten sick, who knows?

My encounter happened the year after they left Joshua Tree early. Our annual family camping trip was coming up but when I asked my parents where they wanted to go, they both said that they didn't want to go camping and they wanted to visit Disney World instead. My brothers were okay with it but I was annoyed with them. I had missed out on Joshua Tree the year before and it had alway been one of my favorite places to go. I told my parents that I wanted to go there and though they tried to dissuade me from doing so, I was eighteen and they couldn't stop me. I asked a few friends and my girlfriend if they wanted to come but each one of them already had something going on and couldn't make it. It was decided that I was going to Joshua Tree alone and my parents and brothers were heading to Florida for Disney World. They left the day before me and I was driving to the park. It would take me about two days and I had my little Ford Explorer so I could pull over and sleep in the back if I needed to. I couldn't drive forty eight straight hours and didn't have the extra money for motel rooms. The trip there was uneventful and once I finally got there all I wanted to do was find a remote location to set up camp and relax. I had one of those tents that zips open on the top so that while you lay inside of it you can look at the stars and the night air flowed through the tent quite nicely. I planned on staying for seven days but that didn't happen. Though they would never admit it, I think the reason why I left early and didn't stay the whole time is the same reason my parents and brothers left early the year before. There was something sinister and terrifying happening in Joshua Tree at that time and mine isn't the only encounter you'll ever find about it all either.

I really don't have an answer to what happened to me out there and I try not to dwell on it. However, more recently I just feel like it's important to tell my story so that people at least become more aware that there are things out there in the world, seemingly in our National Parks areas especially, that just don't make sense. Some of them are very beautiful and some are quite terrifying and possibly deadly and I would warn anyone camping out there, especially if you are alone and purposely isolating yourself, to be extremely careful. Please keep an open mind moving forward because I am the one who experienced this so I am fully aware of how hard to believe it all is. So, it wasn't very crowded and while I was hiking the half hour from my vehicle to where I wanted to set up camp, I had only seen one other hiker. The person looked a little odd and was wearing a black hoodie pulled low down over his face and he had on what looked like black jeans and boots. It was all fairly normal but because it was so mild that day, the way he was all bundled up seemed a bit strange to me. I smiled and said hello as I walked past but the person just stopped in their tracks and seemed to purposely turn their heads from me. They seemed to me like they were trying to make it so I couldn't see their face. Whatever! Live and let live and it takes all types are my mottos in life. I figured they didn't want to chat and went on my way. As I walked away though I got the distinct feeling that whoever it was I had just passed was watching me as I walked away. I got confirmation of this when I turned one more time to look at them and they immediately turned their head away from me again. I was creeped out and started to walk a little faster. It looked like it was about to rain and I decided to stop and set my tent up right next to a gigantic boulder. It was so quiet out there and there was no one else around. I quickly forgot about the weirdo in the hoodie.

I set up my tent and had something to eat and then settled in for the night. It was almost dark out and I was trying to map out what I wanted to do the next day as far as where I would be hiking and things I wanted to see. It was dark before I knew it and I had my bottle of water and flashlight right next to me as I laid down to go to sleep. I was feeling good and nothing seemed out of the ordinary. Not until I woke up in the middle of the night that is. I woke up to what felt like dirt being thrown on me. I jumped up and looked around but immediately thought that perhaps some small animal or another had just been on top of the boulder, which stood several feet higher than my tent and off to the left, and that it had accidentally kicked some debris off of the boulder and into the sky zip on my tent. No big deal and I rolled over onto my side. To explain how I was lying I will say that I was now facing where the boulder was even though I couldn't see it because my tent was in the way. The tent material wasn't very thick but it was enough so that I couldn't see the boulder through it. It had stopped drizzling and now I was much more comfortable. That didn't last long because I saw something move out of my peripheral vision and turned to lay on my back again in order to look up and see what it was. Because I had been lying on my side, my periphery included what was above me, outside of my sky zip.

Looking down on me was the person whom I had passed earlier in the day; the creepy guy who seemed to be hiding his face from me. I couldn't see it any better right then either. He still had the same clothes on and the hood was up. He must have been standing on the boulder because it looked like he was floating there in mid air and I figured that was impossible. I didn't immediately know what to do and thought that maybe the best course of action was to pretend like I hadn't seen him. As soon as I spotted him up there I closed my eyes really quick. I know that sounds ridiculous but the mind is weird when you start to panic and don't know what to do. Once I opened my eyes again though, with every intention of asking the guy what the hell he was doing, he was gone. I was convinced I had only dreamt it but was still a little spooked. I closed the zipper up top on my tent and then realized I had to use the bathroom. I was going to walk into the woods a little bit and do that but I was scared, if I'm being honest. I waited in the tent for a minute or two and intently listened to see if I could hear anyone lurking around out there. I didn't hear anything at all and started to chuckle to myself about how dumb I was being. I should have realized but didn't that it is not normal to hear absolutely nothing in the woods in the middle of the night. I checked my watch and it was about three fifteen in the morning. I peeked out of the front of my tent and looked over towards the boulder- I couldn't believe what I saw.

I literally had to take my hand and cover my own mouth to stop myself from screaming. I was trying not to even breathe for fear that whatever this thing was would see me and do God knows what to me. I was terrified to the very core of my being. I saw what looked like some sort of reptile and human hybrid. It crawled and sort of slithered around on all fours as it moved through the rest of the stuff I had brought with me. Once it got to my backpack that had my clothes in it, which was now a little wet because of the rain, it picked it up and inhaled deeply. It had a look of intense satisfaction on its face that seemed to be due to it sniffing my clothes. I was disgusted and really didn't know what to do. I kept on blinking in the hopes that I was having some sort of hallucination and that none of it was actually happening. I watched as it slithered away and started crawling around on the boulder and then it slithered off into the woods. Before it did so though it turned and looked right at me; right into my eyes, and licked its lips. It had a forked tongue, scaly skin, a human shaped head, bright yellow eyes but they weren't glowing at all. It was like it was all reptile but I somehow knew deep down inside that it was intelligent. I mean, there's no known animal or human being out there that looks like that and I fully believe it was an extraterrestrial. I also believe it had simply been in its human mode or something when I had seen it earlier in the day. I don't know how I knew all of this but I did. That thing knew that I was watching it and it knew that I knew what it really was. I was shocked and all I could do was stare as it turned and went back into the woods. I still had to pee and decided to get out of the tent and go in the opposite direction from where the creature had just gone in order to do so. I planned on being quick and running as fast as I could back to the only safety I had, which was the semi-privacy of my little tent.

My whole body was trembling and as I stepped out of the tent I saw some sort of strange blue light in the sky that looked like it was very deep into the woods. It was in the direction where the creature seemed to have been headed. That's the last thing I remember. I used the bathroom, saw the light when I turned to go back to my tent and that's it. I woke up on the ground right next to my tent the next afternoon. My entire body was sore and I was very confused. I didn't have any memories of what had happened to me and no "nightmares" either. There was a strange mark, like a tiny pin prick, on the inside of my left thigh. I packed up my stuff and hauled ass out of there as fast as I possibly could. I didn't look up the whole time I was walking back to my vehicle because I just knew that I was being watched. My mouth was so dry and my muscles and bones ached. I made it back to my car and got out of there. I drove straight home and when I did have to stop to get some rest I did it in heavily populated areas during the daytime. I wasn't taking any chances. This is the only experience I've ever had with anything alien or paranormal- I still don't know for sure which it was. I was home alone for a little over a week because my family had gone to Florida and I didn't want to ruin their vacation so I waited for them to get home to tell them what happened to me. I didn't speak about it to anyone for fear they would all think I was crazy.

I was very paranoid that whole week. I couldn't sleep and every little sound made me think of the reptilian creature that had been lurking around my campsite. I was driving myself insane and when my family got home I explained to them what I had seen and I told them that I believed I might have been abducted. My mother almost fainted and my father and siblings all turned a ghostly shade of pale. None of them would admit they knew what I was talking about though but I believe that they all had the same encounter the year before when they went to Joshua Tree. My brothers are both still alive and I plan on asking them about it very soon. I want answers but I just don't know where to look other than at everyone else's encounter stories. That's all I know for now but I do believe very much that I was abducted too. I don't know if I ever had any other experiences but I know I have none that I can remember. I've had some nightmares about the creature but I'm not sure if that's so out of the ordinary considering how terrifying it was. I don't go camping anymore and probably won't ever go again. However, I don't think that would stop those beings if they really wanted to get to me or my family again.

SIX

THEY CAME FROM THE FOG

BEFORE I GET STARTED with my encounter I think I should say that I am someone who has always believed there are things in this world that some of us can see and some of us can't. I wholeheartedly believe in ghosts and hauntings and anything supernatural or paranormal will immediately draw me in. The only movies I really watch are horror films, whether they're true stories or not- I just love a good scare. With all of that being said I have to say this runs in my family. My parents don't believe, but my siblings all believe in these things too. I grew up with it, so to speak, and it's always kind of been a part of my life.

While my sisters believe every place we've ever lived has been haunted, I'm more inclined to say that maybe some strange things that we aren't able to understand yet as human beings have happened, sometimes. I'm a believer but I'm not someone who thinks every single unexplainable thing that happens to me or that happens in life in general is paranormal or otherworldly. My encounter happened when some friends and I were just hanging out at a place in the woods near our homes in rural Kentucky in nineteen eighty three. I was sixteen years old and didn't want to spend my time at home doing nothing but would rather spend it out in the woods with my friends so I was at least doing nothing with other people my age. There was a place about a mile up the road from my house that was only accessible by going through some very dense and terribly overgrown woods. It was some structure, it looked to me to be half finished. It was made of brick and had four walls, a space for a door and some small windows but no roof and nothing else. It was strange that it was just out there in the middle of the woods like that but we were all so used to it that we never really questioned why it was there or what it had originally been built for. It seemed to us teenagers that it was some leftover relic from some time long ago and we enjoyed the privacy it lent us.

It had been raining that night and so we covered the

opening at the roof with a large blue tarp that one of us had brought out there at some point in order to do just that. It was only a light drizzle and so it wasn't all that terrible to be out in. I remember the woods seemed to be extra creepy that night, probably because a strange fog had settled over the area where the structure was. We called the structure "the den" and I don't know why it was called that either but that's how we referred to it. Someone long before we were old enough to have made our way out there and made it ours, had written "Welcome to Hell" atop the bricks, right below where the roof should have been. We all thought it was creepy but we weren't vandals and didn't do anything about covering it up. So, the night I had my first encounter with the paranormal my sister Laci and my friend Jean were heading through the forest to meet with our friends Dan and Henry in order to hang out and have a few beers. The boys were bringing the booze and we were bringing ourselves. The five of us sort of had a little clique going and we were outcasts in high school for sure. My sister Laci and Henry were a grade below me and our other two friends, just so you understand the dynamic. We weren't allowed to be at the den or in the woods under any circumstances and it was understood that we would be in a lot of trouble should we get caught there. First of all the entire area of land surrounding the den was private property and had no trespassing signs all over the place. So, it wasn't just that it wasn't permitted by our parents but it was also illegal. We didn't care. Our parents only knew about it because they had hung out there and done the same things in high school.

That night as the three of us walked through the overgrown forest in order to get to the den, a strange fog settled over the area. It was hard to see and we were immediately creeped out. However, we had done that walk so many times that we probably could have done it blindfolded. It wasn't just the fog though it was also the eerie silence that seemed to have settled over the area with it that was really freaking us out. We walked about five miles or so into the woods and it was around seven at night. It had just gotten dark outside too. I know a lot of people will think five miles is a great deal to walk but for us it was like nothing. This was the middle of nowhere in Kentucky in the early eighties. Everything was at least a few miles from everywhere else. Once we got to the den the boys weren't there. We were annoyed because we had specifically waited an extra half hour in order to make sure that we didn't get there first and had to wait for them. It was creepy out there at night and we were only sixteen years old. Laci was almost fifteen but that's besides the point.

After waiting for what seemed like an eternity we

started to hear movement through the fog and it sounded like someone walking. It was like the sound of snapping branches underneath someone's feet. It sounded like more than one person was walking there too. It was so easy to hear because of the aforementioned silence that had pervaded the entire area. We immediately all thought the same thing in that it must be the boys and they were going to try and scare us. We whispered amongst ourselves and made a plan to sneak out of the den where we were all sitting and waiting, and move a little further into the woods behind some trees so we can all jump out at them instead; one after the other. It seemed like a good idea at the time. We all scattered and we had no idea that that was the worst possible thing that we could have done. I went behind a nearby tree that was about ten feet or so from the den and my sister was about five feet behind me, behind another tree. I don't know where Jean went. I heard the sound of walking behind me and thought it was my sister but when I turned around to tell her to get back behind the tree before they saw us, she wasn't there. No one was there and a sickening feeling of dread came over me. I felt like I wanted to scream for some reason. I was scared and at that point nothing had even happened yet. There must've been something inside of me trying to tell me to get out of there but of course I ignored every single instinct I was having in that moment.

Suddenly Jean yelped and came out from her hiding spot which happened to be a few feet to my right. She was cursing and looked really angry. She said she didn't want to hang out anymore and that the boys could go screw themselves. She angrily stormed off into the fog and said she was going home. She didn't even give us a chance to offer to go with her. My sister was giggling and explained that she had crept up behind Jean and grabbed her. Jean hadn't seen her and probably thought the boys did it or that something scary was happening. I found out later on both girls had the same intense and dreadful feelings that I was having but they were also ignoring their guts. I suddenly didn't want to hide anymore and told Laci I just wanted to go home too. The fog was creepy enough but add to it the silence and the footsteps and it was all just too much. There were no cellphones and there was no way to leave a note so we figured we would call the boys when we got home and yell at them for making us go out there, all alone, for nothing. Laci agreed and we decided to let Jean go on her own and she and I would walk by ourselves to let her cool off a bit. That's when the whispering started.

At first I thought it was my sister and I turned and told her that she didn't have to whisper as we weren't hiding anymore. She looked at me with terror in her eyes and a blank stare on her face. She was looking at something behind me, I just knew it. I asked her what her problem was and if she heard the whispering too but all she could do was open her mouth as though she were going to say something but nothing was coming out. She pointed up in the air, behind me. I took a deep breath and turned to look. I remember swearing to myself that if she were in on some prank with the boys or Jean to fool and scare me, I would make her regret it for the rest of her life. I turned around and looked up. There, in the tree about thirty feet above me, there was an extremely tall, pale humanoid creature. It wasn't doing anything but standing there, on the tree and looking at us. I think it was looking at us but it had no eyes or facial features or anything. It was so pale it was almost transparent. The whispering had stopped but it was still eerily quiet. The fog started to lift and I still almost can't believe what happened next.

It's like the fog started turning into those creatures. The tall humanoids just started appearing all over the place until there was no more fog and about ten or twelve of them. Some were on the ground around us and some were standing in the trees above. I honestly don't know if the creatures were the fog or if they just controlled it somehow. I was too terrified to move or say anything. I saw my sister move out of the corner of my eye and when I turned she was gone. She had taken off running and just left me there to fend for myself. She was never as strong as me and I immediately forgave her. I took another look around me and noticed the tall humanoid beings were starting to surround me. I took a step as though to make a run for it but they moved much faster than I had originally anticipated and sort of trapped me in a circle. I was now terrified and crying hysterically. I asked them what they wanted but they didn't respond. However, as I made another move towards them the one in front of me suddenly had a mouth that was gigantic and wide open like a terrifying black, gaping hole and it had the same thing for eyes only smaller. I looked around and it seemed like they all now had these terrifying, open mouthed, dead eyed faces. I started to scream at the top of my lungs because I didn't know what else to do. The creatures responded by all letting out terrifying screeches of delight. They screamed in unison, which made it even more horrifying. They started to close in on me and the few that were in the trees jumped down. I noticed when they landed that they made a thumping sound as though they had some weight to them. I was so confused and kept on thinking that this had to be some sort of nightmare and that I would wake up real soon and laugh at how scared I was. That didn't seem to be happening though.

I covered my ears at the sound of their delightful cackling and yelled again, asking them what they wanted. That's when they all started giggling in unison and it sounded like the giggling of a bunch of five year old girls. I noticed them all moving, very slowly, towards me. They moved strangely. It was like their bodies stretched out as they inched, ever so slowly, closer and closer to me. They had me blocked in and eventually, after who knows how long, they were close enough that had I wanted to I could've reached out and touched them. I thought back to how they seemed to appear from the fog. I closed my eyes and took a deep breath. I then ran as fast as I could. I thought I would have to fight my way out but when I ran towards one of them I went right through it and they all evaporated back into human shaped fog. Then they reformed and the black eyes and black mouths were in the shape of anger. It was almost like a cartoon where now they had sharp eyebrows that formed an "angry" v-shape. I kept running and screaming and thought for sure that they would be coming after me. They didn't though and eventually I made it to the main road. By the time I got home it was after midnight and my parents were, of course, up and waiting for me. It seems as though my sister not only left me there to possibly be killed or abducted, but she also ratted us out to our parents. I was covered in dirt and my clothes were damp and heavy from the foggy mist and light drizzle of rain I spent most of my time that night in. Not to mention I was sweating from running about two miles without stopping at all. I tried to explain to them what I saw but they didn't want to hear it. My mom seemed curious but because dad didn't believe in any of it, I was told to just go to my room. My mom did eventually ask me about it, sometime later, and she said she believed me. It didn't make me feel any better but I've often wondered if maybe she had experienced the same creatures too. I never asked though and she never said anything like that to me. It was just the look on her face when I finally told her everything. My sister said she was sorry as I made my way up to my room. I was grounded for a month. I was still terrified and my mind was still reeling. I needed a shower.

Henry and Dan ended up explaining that they made it as far as a mile into the woods but left because there was too much fog. Jean, after hearing my story, is convinced one of those things grabbed her even though Laci has always admitted to having done it. My sister carried guilt with her for a long time but like I said I forgave her. The entities haunted my dreams and the only way that I can describe them now, as I sit here writing this with all of the memories fresh in my mind still, all these years later, was like the slender man but without clothes. Also, their ever-changing, somewhat comical, black pencil faces. That night wasn't the end of my encounters with the entities though and I truly believe that they are extraterrestrial in nature and have probably abducted me many times since that night. All they ever do anymore is stand and stare. It's like they're there to observe me or something. Beyond that I know absolutely nothing about what their intentions are or where they're from etc.

I often wake up with strange bruises and marks on my body and have ever since that night. I've seen them a handful of times with all but one of them being when I get out of an especially steamy, hot shower. They tend to be lurking in the steam and waiting for me when I get out. It always terrifies me and never seems to get any easier. I saw them one other time, outside of my house when I was twenty years old. They were on my roof and my neighbor's roof and it was raining and misty outside. There was fog. I don't know if all fog everywhere is these entities but I try not to take too many chances and when-ever there will be any sort of weather that leaves even a chance for fog, I stay inside. Again though they visit me there too so that doesn't really help. I don't personally know anyone else who has ever encountered these entities and sometimes I feel like I may be going insane. I wasn't drinking or doing drugs the first night and in fact I don't do any drugs or drink more than socially as an adult. I never have. Maybe I will find similar encounters and I recently found out I don't have much longer to live. I want to try and have at least some of this terrifying puzzle completed before I leave this mortal coil. I'm most terrified that I'll somehow pass it on. My granddaughter Jocelyn has had some pretty frightening and creepy experiences ever since she could talk with all different kinds of entities. I wonder if it's in the genetics and I am so scared because something inside of me says that they will move on to her once I'm gone. All I can do is continue my quest for answers and hope that I'm wrong about that fact. I don't think I am though, it just feels like it's right.

SEVEN

THE LANTERN

WHEN I WAS a teenager back in 1979, I worked at a state park. I was on the maintenance team and usually worked during the day shift. However, the 4th of July weekend was supposed to be very busy with campers and they needed me to help work the camper registration. I did, and found it enjoyable. It also was where I met my girlfriend at the time, but that is another story entirely.

I worked until the camp office closed at midnight but instead of me clocking out, the night ranger wanted me to go clean some of the showers and bathrooms before I left. It had been busy already and people had already trashed them.

I agreed and made my way to the showers via a short trail.

Now I should take the time to detail a bit about the park. It had one been a part of the Natchez Trail and there was a lot of history about the area that dated back to the Native Americans.

I made my way to the showers and bathrooms on this trail, a trail I had taken often, but never at night. I wasn't one to get spooked so I didn't think much of walking in the dark.

I made a turn on the trail, I should note I was using a flashlight, not a bright one, but enough that I could see the trail. Ahead of me I saw a light, I thought it was a camper and didn't think much of it until I noticed the light had a weird color, like it was more orangey and flickered like it was a flame. I stopped and looked more carefully to see that it definitely was a flame and it appeared to be behind glass, this was a lantern. I shrugged it off as campers had lanterns. I proceeded ahead but as I drew closer to the lantern, which bobbed up and down and swung left to right, I noticed there wasn't anyone holding it. The light given off from the lantern was bright enough to see around it and it was evident, no one was there. It was as if the thing was hovering on its own. I took a pause, lifted my flashlight and boom my suspicions were confirmed, there was no one there, I saw the lantern and then it was gone. I lowered my flashlight quickly to spot the light from the lantern only to confirm it was gone. I raised my flashlight again and looked around but saw no one and no lantern.

The hairs on my neck rose and goosebumps covered my skin. What had I seen. Again, not one who got spooked easily, I continued on to the showers and did my job.

The next day at work I mentioned to my supervisor what I'd seen. He chuckled and told me I was one of the lucky few who had seen the floating lantern.

I asked him what it was and he promptly told me that people had been seeing it for a century or more. That there were reports dating way back. I asked him who it might be and he gave me several different possibilities with one being an old trapper who lived in the area. That his wife had been abducted my Natives and he went searching for her only to get killed himself. He said the old trapper now spends eternity searching for his wife.

Creepy and cool all at the same time. I worked at the park for a few more months and never saw the lantern again.

EIGHT

I CAN STILL SEE IT LOOKING AT ME

I'LL ADMIT I feel awkward sending this e-mail as the people I've told have mocked me.

Anyway here goes. I grew up on a farm in southern Maryland and we had over a hundred of acres of mostly wooded land. Our property was adjacent to other large swaths of heavily wooded acreage.

To cut to the chase, I was an avid hunter growing up. So much that during my teens I'd go squirrel hunting daily after getting home from school.

One afternoon in October I went out alone. I was 16. However this time I decided to go further into the woods. As I hiked along my mind was somewhere else until I noticed I was in a part of the woods I'd never been to. I was surrounded by old growth trees and the terrain was rolling hills. I looked down into the bottom of this hollow and saw large grove of laurel. I slowly made my way down and suddenly was overcome with a heavy feeling of dread and that I was being watched. So much that I froze and began to look around expecting to see another person but didn't.

This fear kept growing to the point that I felt terror for lack of a better word. Without notice I saw movement in the laurel. Footfalls and branch snapping.

I called out that I wasn't alone hoping that whoever was in there would stop trying to scare me.

The footfalls stopped but my fear was still high. I was armed with a Ruger 77/22 bolt action rifle. I leveled the rifle at the laurel and again called out for whoever was in there to know I wasn't alone.

Then a chattering almost laughter came from the laurel bushes. It was so weird, it sounded like a cackle. Filled with fear I fired my rifle above the laurel.

Then all hell broke loose. The laughter became a growl. And the laurel was crashing. I could see that from the top of the bushes that it was coming towards me.

I again called out and again fired. It didn't stop.

I turned and ran up the slope. Now I should

mention that it was dusk, the light was going fast and by how far I'd gone I wouldn't get back to my house until after dark.

When I crested the top of the hill I looked back and saw something hairy step out of the laurel and look up at me. Now as I write this I'm getting a chill up my spine.

I can still see it looking at me.

I cycled the bolt on the rifle and fired at it. I missed as it didn't respond, it stepped fully out and stood up. Whatever it was wasn't huge it was about five to six feet tall. I know, it doesn't sound like a Bigfoot but it had wide shoulders, long arms and covered in hair.

I took off as fast as I could, I was in a panic, I kept falling down and tripping. I was getting shredded by branches hitting my face but I didn't care. I could hear whatever it was chasing me. It was barreling through the woods but not directing behind me. What's odd is it seemed to be running parallel to me.

After 15 minutes I could see the lights of my house through the trees and this thing was still running near me. The issue I had was that if I turned right to head to the trail to go to my house I'd encounter this thing, so I passed the trail and headed around the trail and out into the field.

When I was in the field, I was screaming for my

family, I turned and cycled the bolt and fired into the woods again. It was dark now completely.

I listened but heard nothing but I could sense it was still there. I ran to the house and went inside.

When I encountered my mom I was crying and covered in blood from all the cuts and slashes in my face.

My older brother grabbed a shotgun and went out, I followed him with a fully loaded rifle. And it should be said this was against my mother's wishes.

We both fired into the woods, and yelled at whatever it was.

I never encountered it again and I didn't go hunting by myself, nor have I ever ventured too far into the woods alone since.

My mother didn't believe me, she thought it was probably a black bear and my other siblings made fun of me. However my grandmother who lived in a house on the farm for 55 years told me she'd seen stuff years before and even had seen lights above the forest years back, but that's an entirely different story.

Thank you, it feels good to get this off my chest.

NINE

THE EVENT

MY WIFE and I had our crazy event in 1978 and it's still something that I'm processing through, I never saw a therapist, but have often thought I probably should have.

My wife and I had always referred to our encounter as "the event", when we discussed it in private. Our children don't have a clue about the event and I'd like to keep it that way. My wife has since passed and I don't think it wise they're aware, so thank you for allowing me to share with discretion and privacy.

So, with all of that out of the way, let's me tell you about it:

Our "event" took place in late November 1978 in the Pennsylvania countryside. The county had just built a new park that had a few baseball fields, a playground and tennis courts surrounded by woods, a nice creek and a whole lot of farmland around it. On Friday and Saturday nights, the new park became a very popular spot for high school kids to go and "park" or just hang out and party in the small pavilion there when the weather was mild. It quickly became a favorite spot for my then girlfriend, and soon to be wife.

The evening of our encounter was a cold one and we had the car running, heat on and the perfect music playing on my eight track. I had just backed my recently purchased 1969 Nova SS in the closest parking spot near the woods so no one could see us from the main road. We were the only car in the lot that night. I think because it was so cold out. We hadn't been there very long, maybe 15-20 minutes. We were talking and laughing when a large number of deer came running behind our car. We heard a huffing sound, and thought it was the deer, but soon we'd discover it was something else.

They were really moving, and I'd never seen deer run like that before. We'd always see them in the fields, just grazing and maybe looking up when a car pulled into the lot. About a minute later, there was a small thud on the trunk of the car.

I said to my girlfriend, "It's probably just one of the deer".

Almost immediately after I said that there was a big thud. It was enough that it moved the car up and down one time. This was significant because the weekend before, we had gone to a friend's party and had pulled up on the curve where the party was being held. A few of my football buddies ran up and started pushing down on the trunk to make the car wobble up and down. I jumped out and chased them. It was all good fun, and we were all laughing. Just a stupid high school thing. So, immediately I thought my buddies had spotted us from the road somehow as they drove by, snuck up on us and was messing with us again. I jumped out to chase them and had my long maglite flashlight, the same that cops use. I was expecting to see a group of teenagers with wide shit-eating grins, but what I found myself staring at was the face of something that doesn't or shouldn't exist. At that exact moment, my girlfriend spotted out the back window the same thing I was looking at and began screaming.

It was just enormous, ugly and it was obviously not happy. I'm pretty sure it was already growling when I opened my car door and jumped out. It was a low growl, but it was a growl I've never forgotten. It rumbled my chest, like a bass guitar would at a 70s rock concert. It was very strange that it was such a low volume, but I could still feel it intensely in my body.

It was only about five to six feet away from me and it had saliva dripping from its mouth. Its eyes look reddish, maybe a dark orange and they appeared to be glowing. I've never been sure if it was a reflection, or they were self-illuminating. At the time, I was 6'3" and weighed 225 and found myself staring up at it, I think it had to be nine to ten feet tall if not taller and had to weigh well over 400lbs. I felt very small, like a child would next to a pro-football lineman. The thing was incredibly bulky, massive and intimidating in a way I'd never known before or since. It's also amazing how fast your mind moves at a moment like that.

The entire encounter outside the car was only a few seconds long. As it took off at a speed and with such a grace that seemed supernatural. As if it were wearing skates, it seemed to glide away. It's hard to explain, but it was towering over me one second and the next it's hauling ass away, each footfall thundered and was twelve feet apart from the next.

As it made its move, I made mine and jumped back

in the car. My girlfriend was still screaming hysterically, but what sounds odd is her voice seemed distant, like she was a mile away. I can't recall each following second or even putting the car into gear, but I did as I vividly recall driving over the grass barrier and onto the main road at a speed so fast the car lurched heavily to the left, almost putting the car on two wheels.

As my girlfriend continued to scream I started to ask, "What the hell was that! What the hell was that!" at the top of my lungs over and over again. I slammed my foot against the accelerator once the car righted itself and sped down the road, I must have been going close to 100 miles per hour. Eventually my girlfriend touched my arm and told me to slow down.

I left off the gas and pulled off at the Waffle House near town. We both sat in the parking lot, neither saying a word to the other. I looked up at the Waffle House sign and suddenly felt an urge to eat. I know it sounds odd, but I was starving. I told her I needed to eat and got out of the car. I was on autopilot, and without thinking about her, I just went inside.

She quickly followed, the entire time peppering me with questions. But I ignored her and simply ordered a large breakfast of eggs, bacon, and toast. All I could think about was food. I can't explain it, but when the plate came, I devoured the food and wanted more. Maybe it was some sort of survival thing, I had lived through something so traumatic that my body needed the nourishment. Who knows. She didn't order anything and said she didn't have an appetite. She simply sat across from me in the booth and kept asking me question for which I didn't answer.

It took me a month before I would actually talk with her about it. All we could think was it was a Bigfoot, but I never thought at the time they were in Pennsylvania, I thought they lived in the Pacific Northwest. What was a Sasquatch doing out east, had it gotten lost? I know that question seems silly, but my teenager brain didn't know anything about these creatures then.

We both agreed to not discuss nor disclose what we'd seen and the reason was simple, people wouldn't believe us and they'd think we were crazy. Plus, I needed to get my scholarship to college and what school would give one to a kid who saw 'Bigfoot'. I didn't want to risk my future so we kept it to ourselves.

Many years later we did tell friends, but that brief mention got us scorn and ridicule. It's so strange how you can't tell people such things without receiving a ton of pushback. So here I am, my wife has passed, my kids are grown and I'm telling you this, but like I said, I still have fear of ridicule, so this story, this event will be anonymous.

I know what we saw that night. We hadn't been drinking. We didn't do drugs. We saw something out of nightmares. It exists, Bigfoot exists.

TEN

DOGMAN IN THE DEEP WOODS

IN DOING research on all things, "dogman", since I had my encounter back in 1999, I have come across so many different creatures- it's insane. From werewolves to Bigfoot-like creatures to shapeshifters and skinwalkers, the one thing I haven't come across is anything similar to what I saw back then.

All I can say is I saw an actual dog-man; half dog and half man. It was grotesque yet fascinating. It was terrifying, yet I couldn't turn away from it. Let me start at the beginning. I was out for a simple walk around my neighborhood. I lived in a very wooded area in southern New Jersey. There are parts around the area where I live that are well known for terrifying creatures and unusual cryptids. There are woods all along the backs of the houses and one night I just decided to go into the woods and take the trails. I would come out the other side about an hour later and it wouldn't be any different than the dozen other times I had done the same thing. Well, at least that's what I initially thought. I like to go on nightly walks, it was something I had been doing since I was much younger. I grew up in Washington State and to say that New Jersey is like a whole different place would be an understatement. It's more like it's a whole different planet. I was relocated for work in nineteen ninety seven and was just starting to get adjusted two years later when I had my encounter with the creature in the woods. Whenever I would miss my family or my old home, I would take the detour through the woods during my nightly walk instead of sticking to the main roads. I am a guy but I still carried mace with me and I always had a flashlight too.

I started my walk like usual and was sticking to the sidewalks but I felt very exposed. I think something was drawing me into the woods, though I wasn't aware of it at the time. I have always been an avid hunter and experienced woodsman and I wasn't worried at all when I would take the walk through the woods near my home. I wouldn't describe them as extremely dense or anything but there was one spot in the middle of them that always made me feel at peace and like I was in one of the dense and unending forests back in Washington. I lived in a very low crime neighborhood and there weren't even very many bears out at that time of year. I turned into one of the neighbors driveways down the street from my house, made my way through their yard and went into the woods. My neighbors didn't care at all and it was normally by this route that I would go into the woods. They had a full trail leading from their backyard and all the way through to the other side of the woods and they were one of the only homes in the area that had one. It was really thick and overgrown most other places, including when trying to enter into them from my own yard. I would always stop in the middle and sit on a particular, large boulder and watch and listen to the water run. It ran off the reservoir that stood where I would eventually end up coming out of the woods.

The woods immediately felt different that night. There was a strange calm and it seemed like it was more quiet than it usually was or even than it should have been. It wasn't so bad that it scared me or anything and I made it to the boulder without any issues. I did feel like I was being intensely watched from the moment I entered the woods but I was going through a lot, both personally and professionally, at the time and figured it was just my over-anxious mind playing tricks on me. I sat down and all was calm and normal for the first five minutes or so that I was sitting there. I started to hear what sounded like faint howling, like it was coming from far away. Now, it wasn't unusual for there to be coyotes in that particular area but it was strange in that it sounded like they were coming from SO far away and like I said earlier, there wasn't much to these woods. It was a small patch of them, when compared to the other surrounding areas. These were woods I could walk into, through and back out of in the matter of an hour or so. I shrugged it off. I sat in quiet contemplation for another ten minutes or so. I started hearing what sounded like heavy breathing accompanied by sticks and branches snapping- as though under someone or something's feet. The hairs on the back of my neck and on my arms immediately stood up. I turned to look around but I was suddenly dizzy. I leaned forward in order to stop the world from seeming to spin around me. I was nauseous and starting to think I was maybe having a heart attack or at the very least a panic attack .

I had my head down between my legs and my eyes

closed but I knew that there was something close by now and I figured it wasn't a human being. I knew that I had to get up and cautiously look around before getting out of there. I picked up my head and some of the dizziness subsided but I was still sweating profusely and shaking uncontrollably. This had never happened to me before and I think at the time I was more scared of what was happening with my body than with whatever I thought I would end up facing by the end of it. I had no way of knowing my worst nightmare was about to come true. You see, I am a horror movie collector and have seen probably close to every single one ever made, in the history of horror movies. It never escaped my notice that a lot of strange and terrifying things happened in woods just like the ones I was then sitting in. I figured I needed to get up and start moving. It would take a lot longer to continue the path to the reservoir than it would for me to just turn around and go back the way that I came and so I chose the latter option. First I decided, while my legs were still shaky at best, to shine my flashlight around me and see if I could spot anything. I still wasn't connecting whatever was lurking around me with how sick I was getting at that moment. It took me a very long time to make that connection too.

I shined my flashlight all around the area despite not hearing anything anymore. There was nothing but silence and the sound of my own heavy breathing. As I stopped to listen one more time before making my exit though, I started to hear the heavy breathing again- it wasn't mine that time. I looked around but still the flashlight didn't illuminate anything. I turned to walk away and that's when I heard the strangest noise. It sounded like the grunting of a dog but it was also like a human moaning in pain. It was the strangest thing I've ever heard in real life. Still I couldn't see anything. I turned back around just to make sure that nothing had crept up behind me as whatever it was sounded really close by. That's when I thought that I had seen something move but it looked like it was moving near a small bear cave across the water. So it was close enough, whatever it was, but it would have had to cross the water to get to me. Considering it was a bear cave I assumed it was a bear. Water isn't a deterrent for bears by any means and so I decided to get the hell out of there. I tried to move quickly but without running. I shone my flashlight across the water one more time and that's when I saw what it was that had not only been watching me since I had sat down there on the large boulder, but what I'm sure had probably had its eyes on me since the moment I stepped into the woods through my neighbor's yard or possibly even sooner. It just stood there, right out in the open and not even trying to hide from my flashlight.

It was grotesque. It had a long snout like a canine and looked to be the breed of a German shepherd. It had long fangs and it was slobbering all down its chin and chest. It stood on two legs like a human being and seemed to have a human chest, arms and legs too. It was covered in short black fur. Its ears were like that of a dog and its hands and feet were more like paws- albeit giant ones. This is what I recognize now as a dogman. It was literally half dog and half man. It was snarling and salivating. Its eyes were a yellowish orange that almost reflected the light from the flashlight back onto it. I just stood there perfectly still and stuck on stupid wondering what in the hell I was staring at and what in the world I was going to do about it. Something about its stance made me feel like it was threatening and/or challenging me. I was prepared to turn and run. It's almost as though it read my mind because as soon as I thought that- to turn and run- it let out a massive and incredibly loud, inhuman or half human, maybe, howl. It got down on all fours and I knew in that moment if I didn't get a hold of myself and make a run for it then this thing was going to get across the water faster than I had originally anticipated when it was standing there on its two legs, and more than likely I was going to be killed. It possibly wanted to make a meal out of me but I was thinking at that moment that maybe it was some sort of werewolf hybrid and maybe I would then become one of them. I have since looked at that night on the internet to see if it was a full moon out or not. There was no full moon on that night and in fact it was three days waning.

I turned and ran and immediately heard a splash in the water. I kept telling myself not to look back, even when I heard it so close behind me that it seemed as though it would take one final leap and be on me. Suddenly I heard it yelp and it was a very loud yelp and as though it had somehow hurt itself or was otherwise in a lot of pain for whatever reason. I turned around just in time to see it flying through the air. I didn't even want to know what happened. Something must have gotten a hold of it and sent it flying ten feet in the air, backwards and away from me. I still don't know what happened but whatever it was, it more than likely is what saved my life. I made it to my neighbor's yard and ran through it like a bat out of hell. I didn't even bother with opening their fence and just hopped over it. I got to the sidewalk of the main road and walked the rest of the few blocks to my house in silence. I was having trouble catching my breath and still couldn't wrap my mind around what I had just seen and been confronted with. I was looking around me the whole way home and kept thinking that that thing, whatever it was, was now more pissed off than ever and waiting in the wings somewhere to come out and grab me. I had nightmares for months and it took me years before I would even walk the main roads at night again.

I didn't start to research it all right away. It took me a few years before I would even start to come to terms with it and even more time before I felt ready to talk about it. I was careful who I would mention it to. When I brought it up to some of the neighbors who I had gotten to know even better over the years, they all looked at me like I was crazy. I always made it like I was only kidding and with them knowing how into horror movies and that type of stuff I was, they would laugh it off. I still live in the same house and still walk the same streets and have even recently started walking those same paths in the woods again. I never saw it again but I get a feeling sometimes that I'm being watched or stalked. Maybe I'm even being hunted but this time it's taking its time with me for fear that whatever happened to it last time, which I'm still confused about and had absolutely nothing to do with, will happen to it again. I hope it keeps right on thinking that. I may bring my pistol with me one night and try to just shoot whatever it is, who knows? That's it for now but if I come across it or anything else again, I'll write another encounter story. This is what the dogman is. At least in my opinion and I'm sure I'm not the only one out there who has seen such a creature but based on how I was treated and the responses I got when I would tell people about what I saw, I'm not surprised there aren't too many people coming forward with these kinds of sightings.

ELEVEN

THE COMMUTE

I HAD an experience that left me feeling a little crazy and confused. I wasn't a believer but once you see something like I did, you can't ever get it out of your mind and it forever changes you.

Let me tell you about myself first. I'm 31, have three kids and I'm married to a wonderful down to earth woman. I'm originally from San Diego and moved to the Columbus, Ohio area about nine months ago so my wife could be closer to family and we could escape the rat race. I took a job as a mechanic at a local car dealership (I don't want to mention which). The job means I have to commute about an hour each day.

When I leave my house it's always dark and I'll admit I'm fine with that, the drive is rather boring, but there's never any traffic. It allows me to listen to some podcasts, I'm really into many that deal with self-improvement, so I look at the commute as a time I get to literally improve myself.

The morning in question is a day I'll never forget. I'm up at my usual time which is 4:30. I pack my lunch, grab my coffee and head out. I distinctly recall it being cold out, like freezing temperatures because I slipped on our front steps and almost went down hard. Thank goodness I have cat like reflexes.

The drive was normal, nothing to write home about as they say until I saw it, at first I thought my eyes were playing tricks on me. It was a large mass, but in reality it was this huge human like being standing along the side of the road. If anyone has driven around central Ohio they can confirm that many roads are flat and straight, they go on for mile after mile like this. There's literally nothing else out there, not much in the way of trees or shrubs, yet there was this large black mass which as I drew closer looked like a human in a fur suit.

I began to slow because I wasn't sure if this person needed help or was going to commit suicide by car. The last thing I wanted was to run over someone. But as I drew closer and closer, I started to get a feeling this wasn't a person in a fur / monkey suit, but something else, something scary. With my spidey senses on high alert, I pulled the car into the opposite lane (it was a two-lane highway), to give myself as much distance as I could between me and it.

As I was finally coming up on the thing I now got a good look at it and there was no way this was a man wearing any kind of suit, this thing was huge and tall and I could feel its stare. I felt like it was looking into my soul.

The second I had that feeling I smashed my foot on the gas. My car lurched forward but not fast enough for my liking. It stood there just starting at me, then I saw the other thing that scared me, in its right hand, which was facing away from me, was the head of deer.

It looked like the head had been ripped off, as the edges on the neck were uneven. On the ground underneath the head was the body, its abdomen ripped open, guts splayed out and a large pool of blood. Had this thing killed the deer or was it just eating roadkill?

I don't know what I was looking at. It's just strange to see something that's out of a nightmare or taken from a horror movie. My brain was having a difficult time processing what my eyes were seeing. I recall my heart was racing and I had this intense feeling of dread. I was terrified and unsure if this thing would make a move on my car. Just as I passed the creature made a quick motion as if it might toss the deer head at me. I swerved onto the shoulder of the road, my tires spun and for a second I almost lost control of my car. My rapidly beating heart almost exploded. I managed to get control of my car and slammed my foot down hard. I looked into the rearview mirror, but it was too dark to see anything.

I got to work and felt as if I'd run a marathon. I was exhausted, no doubt due to the emotional stress my encounter had given me. All day I thought about the creature, and I wondered if I'd see it on my way home.

Speaking of my drive home, when I passed the spot all there was on the side of the road was a large spot caused by the blood. There was no sign of the deer carcass or the creature. I was tempted to pull over, but I thought it best not to tempt fate, so I continued on.

It's been a few months since I and each morning I'm alert and ready for another encounter, but I've never seen the thing since.

TWELVE

NIGHT VISITOR

THE FOLLOWING ISN'T my personal story or encounter but was told to me by my grandfather some years ago before he passed away. The last time he detailed it to me I made sure to record him and write it down as I found it interesting and scary. I never thought I'd be sharing it, but here goes.

———

My grandfather worked from the late 1960s to the mid 1970s as an engineer in Wyoming. When he told me this story, he was a bit foggy on the exact dates, but the other details seemed vivid and on point.

The project he was working on was just outside of Jackson which is near the Tetons. It's a beautiful area, picturesque, if you've never been, I highly recommend visiting one day. He wasn't from Jackson, he and my grandmother lived in Cheyenne, so this was to be a remote job and would take him about three weeks.

He was on the job for a week and things were already falling behind so he decided to stay on the job site until he could get caught up. This required him to possibly spend the night. They had set up a camper on the site for just this reason, but no one had needed it until now.

The job site was remote, located on the edge of a national forest and my grandfather said it was one of the most beautiful places he'd ever visited. He described it as pristine, just as God had made it.

Well, the day turned to night and under the light of a gas lantern he worked. He made himself food earlier but found he wasn't that hungry so he left it sitting out near the fire while he was in the camper going over engineering sketches or whatever it was he was doing.

He said he heard some movement outside, like someone was walking around. He peeked through a window but couldn't see a thing. He ignored the sound and went back to work only to be disturbed by rustling near the fire, he got up from where he was sitting and looked through a window which faced the fire and said he saw something hunched over next to the fire next to where he left his plate. He thought it was a bear and didn't want it staying around so he was thought he should scare it off. He quickly opened the door, but before he could holler for it to go away, it had taken off into the woods. He could hear it crashing as it went. He saw the plate on the ground and the food was gone. He picked it up, laughed it off and went back to work.

He grew tired, but before he went to bed, he wanted to just relax by the fire and enjoy the stars. The night he said was moonless so the light show, as he called it, would be fantastic. As he relaxed, a whiskey in his hand he looked up and took it the splendor. He told how he'd get mesmerized by the stars out west, he said nowhere back east can touch the night sky of the upper Rocky Mountains; he was biased of course, but after having visited Wyoming myself to visit, I can say I agree.

So, he said he was just relaxing and taking it all in when a feeling of being watched came over him. He said it was so intense that he sat up and looked around. He felt like he wasn't alone and began to wonder if the 'bear' was around. He had cleaned up any food so that couldn't be it, but then again, he thought, if a bear is hungry and found food before they could be coming back for more. One thing he didn't know then that we know now is bears to cruise around in the middle of the night, they're more day trippers.

As he looked around, he couldn't shake the feeling. He got so spooked that he went to the trailer and got his Smith and Wesson .357 revolver. While he wasn't one to spook too easily, he also was a realist and having already dealt with a visitor earlier, he wasn't about to become bear food or at the minimum he'd not go quietly and without a fight.

Back at the fire, whiskey in one hand and the revolver in his lap; he went back to enjoying the evening. He said it was a cool and crisp late summer evening and the fire gave him just the warmth he needed. As he sat there proud of what he'd accomplished that day and having already forgotten about the 'bear' and the odd feeling, he began to get sleepy. He nodded a few times, then a loud snap, like that of a large branch breaking jogged him awake. He sat up and looked around, spilling his whiskey in the process.

Again, that feeling of being watched came over him. Was someone out there? He called out, but didn't get a reply, not that he was expecting one. He sat his whiskey down on the ground and went to stoke the fire which had began red hot embers, but just before doing so he thought he should call it a night and get a good night's rest. He got up and went to the camper.

He got in bed and just as he was dozing off, he said he heard heavy footfalls near the fire pit. He sat up, peered through the window but couldn't see anything. He couldn't shake the feeling he had before, and now he had another feeling, one of dread. He hadn't taken his revolver to bed with him, but just in case; he got up, took it from the table where he'd left it sitting out and brought it back to bed. As he laid there, he said he could hear someone walking around the camper. Their footfalls were distinct and notably heavy. He said that word a good number of times, so I knew just how unusual the footfalls sounded.

Was someone out there? Did he want to confront them or just leave it be? It wasn't like they could really steal anything. He decided he'd just leave it be and go to bed. He pressed his eyes closed but each time he began to drift he'd heard the walking and a flood of nervous energy would come over him. Frustrated, he got up and went to go holler at whoever or whatever was out there. He said when he threw the door open, he saw something, a dark shape near the fire pit, he said it was crouching where he left his glass of whiskey and when he opened the camper door, it stood and faced him. It was then he appreciated the height of this thing. Something my grandfather made a point I heard. He said it must have been eight feet tall and was built like a brick shithouse. He and it were in a Mexican standoff for what seemed like an eternity, before it gave up, turned took off. He said the thing moved fast, like watching someone run on a recording that was sped up one and half times. Like before he heard crashing through the forest, branches cracking and breaking.

My grandfather was officially scared. First what on earth was this thing and could it come back and possibly hurt him? He closed the door to the camper and sat for a moment thinking about what he should do. He was tempted to leave, but was that smart? He gave it a few more minutes and decided that he loved his wife, my grandmother, too much to hang out and possibly be this thing's next meal. He grabbed his stuff, had his revolver, and went for the work truck which was parked just outside of the camper.

He fired up the truck and turned on the headlights to see the thing had returned and was standing on the edge of the woods near the fire pit. It was looking right at him. With the headlights on it, he got a good look. He reiterated its height and said it was covered in a thick brown fur or hair which was matted in certain spots, and it had twigs, leaves and branches stuck in its hair. He said its face resembled a mix between a cave man, like

Neanderthal and gorilla. It wasn't really an ape but it also wasn't a man. It stood on two legs and had really long arms. He said he only saw one arm, its left as the other was hidden behind a small pine tree.

He had seen enough, he put the truck into gear, his hands shaking and backed up. After turning the wheel hard to the left and freeing up his right hand, he picked up the revolver and had it ready just in case the thing wanted to try 'something funny', those were his words. He sped down the dirt road, hitting every pothole. His heart raced and he kept peering into the rearview mirror expecting to see the thing making chase, but he saw nothing.

He made it back to his hotel room an hour later and was still shaking by the experience. He couldn't go to sleep and instead waited up. He met the others in the hotel lobby where they'd get coffee and a donut before heading out to the job site. They asked why he was there and not out at the job site. He didn't lie, my grandfather was a man of integrity and told them everything. Every detail to a tee.

At first they took him serious and listened intently then after he was done they laughed it off and gave him the typical pats on the back and gave him credit for coming up with a great doozy of a story or asked him how much had he drank or if he was doing the 'whacky tobacky'. He was adamant that he was telling them the truth, but they had none of it.

He and the crew went out to the job site and found not only their equipment, but the camper had been messed with. Trash and debris were strewn all over. They instantly wanted to blame my grandfather, but then they discovered the huge footprints all over the place. Their joking had turned to accusations then to dismay as some believed my grandfather was telling the truth.

The owner of the company pulled him aside and flat out asked him if he had done this. My grandfather denied doing the damage and once more told him what had happened.

His boss paused and decided right then and there to believe him. He had known my grandfather for a long time, and not once in those years working together had he seen this type of behavior. All he and his men could do was believe my grandfather.

They cleaned up the camper and the work site. The equipment wasn't destroyed, just some dings and dents, but nothing beyond repair or taken out of commission. The air around the job site that day was filled with a weariness, and everyone was looking over their shoulders half expecting to see a monster emerge from the woods and attack them.

When the day wrapped up, they all loaded in the trucks and left. No one volunteered to remain, and they made sure there was no food or anything that an animal would find enticing.

Upon their return the next day the site was untouched although they did find some fresh tracks around the camper. New tracks continued to appear for a few more days than nothing. Whatever my grandfather saw was gone.

My grandfather stuck by this story until the very end. About two weeks before he passed away, my wife reminded me to bring it up again with hopes of finally documenting it on a recorder so I could write it down.

I asked him, "Grandpa, remember the story about the monster in Wyoming?"

He looked at me, smiled and said, "Of course."

I asked, "Did you embellish at all?"

He stoically replied, "No, there was no reason to. It happened the way I said it happened."

I took his hand and squeezed. I said, "I believe you grandpa."

He passed away not long after that. I'm happy I got his voice on that recording and wrote this story down so it may be shared. I feel like a little piece of him lives on. He was a great man, an adventurer of sorts. I can still see him sitting out underneath the stars, a whiskey in one hand and his revolver in the other. There's not a time I don't look up at the stars and think of him and that story. I know now he had a run in with a Sasquatch, a creature many say doesn't exist, well I know my grandfather would never lie and even though I've never seen one, I don't need to in order to believe.

THIRTEEN

THEY WANTED OUR BLOOD

I GREW up in a family with just my father and four brothers. My mother died when I was really young and so from a very young age on upward I kind of became just one of the boys. Everything my dad and brothers did I did as well and I thought it was the greatest thing in the world. My father was somewhat of what we would call nowadays a survivalist, I guess. He stocked canned goods and water, things like that, out on our ten acre property. It was huge and he even had a storm shelter built that looked almost like an underground bunker except it wasn't underground. My dad took that type of stuff seriously but my brothers and I were always a little embarrassed by it. He was a great dad though and we always had a lot of fun together as a family. I was a surprise baby, I guess you could say, and I was quite a bit younger than my siblings. There came a point in time where they were all off doing their own thing; preteens and teenagers, and I was left to hang by myself when they were out doing whatever and my dad was working. This happened back in the late seventies and it wasn't unusual for someone to leave a young child home alone. We lived in a very secluded, rural and isolated area of Alabama and very near to our property, somewhat attached to it actually, there was a very large swamp area. I always felt right at home there and would often travel through the dense woods on the large property where I lived to hang out by myself. I would wander around and play pretend. I loved the outdoors and still do to this very day. Despite everything I've witnessed in my time living in that house and traversing through the surrounding wooded areas. Now that you have a little bit of background, let me get into my encounter story.

It was a day not unlike any other really. The only difference was that the night before it had rained very hard and there was a strange lightning storm in the sky. What I mean when I describe it like that is that it was strange for Alabama at the time. The sky lit up with regular, though very brightly colored, lightning. It was scary and the wind whipped the rain around like crazy. It was unlike anything I had ever seen before but there were also these strange lights that seemed to be coming from nowhere in the sky that I would see every so often as I looked out the window to watch the insane storm that was swirling all around outside. The beams of light looked like they were shining down randomly into the woods with particular attention being paid to the area where the swamp was. Obviously I stayed inside that day and night but I slept well to the sounds of the storm and the next day the sun was shining again. I put on my mud boots, as we called them, and dressed in my regular clothing that I would wear when out exploring in the woods and swamp areas. My brothers had all gone somewhere or another and my dad had to work an overnight shift. I stayed out all day and when I came home for dinner it was just me and my dad. Everything was fine but when I tried to ask him questions about the night before I noticed he kept changing the subject. I thought it was weird but didn't worry about it too much. He left after making me promise I would go no further than the bunkers and not go exploring in the woods or the swamp area. Now, I had been out in those woods and around that swamp all day and he hadn't said anything. I was very frustrated because I wanted to go in the night and see if there was anything that would lend a clue as to what those lights were. Science fiction movies and books were very popular at the time and I had it in my head that they had been alien related. My dad said I was nuts and that there were no such things as UFOs or aliens but I thought deep down he knew something he wasn't telling me. After a little bit of arguing back and forth I finally agreed to stay within the area of the house and the bunkers, if I were to go outside at all. I meant to keep that promise, I really did.

I had no interest in exploring what was basically my backyard. After all, I had done that millions of times and the lights hadn't been beaming down in that area. I planned on just settling in with a good, scary book and calling it a night. I had a fairly uneventful evening until around two in the morning when I had to take my dog out for his final business before I went to bed. I always went to bed late during the summer and this wasn't anything unusual. I never used a leash and this time was no different. I let him out and he ran and sniffed around a little bit. I wasn't in a rush and we were out there for about five minutes when I saw the lights in the woods again. This time they weren't shining from the sky down into the woods but seemed to be just shining somewhere inside of the woods; hovering. I wanted so badly to go and check it out and investigate but I knew how much trouble I would be in once my dad got home. He always knew, somehow, what I had been up to when he was gone. I guess I was just a really bad liar and normally I would just tell on myself. However, when my dog saw the lights he went barreling towards the woods. I called for him to come back but he didn't even turn around. I had no choice but to run after him. Before I knew it I was in the woods, my dog was nowhere in sight and I had no idea where I was. It was like everything was different and I couldn't manage to get my bearings on where I had entered the woods or how far inside of them I was. I had to find my dog and kept calling his name over and over again. I received no response. I kept walking further into the woods until finally I knew I was really far away from my house because I was at the swamp. I worried that he had accidentally run into the swampy water and wouldn't come back out. I certainly couldn't go in and get him. I didn't know what to do and had to stop for a moment and think about it.

Just as I stopped I heard what sounded like my dog yelping in pain and then whining. He was somewhere nearby. I called out to him again and he came to me. He was limping though and bleeding from his back left leg. He looked pitiful and his fur was all ratted up. It looked like someone had roughly picked him up by his scruff- sort of like you do with young kittens or cats- and had done something to him. He came to me for a moment but kept on limping right past me. He was a small dog and I went to pick him up. He growled at me the moment I went to grab him and he actually bit me. He bit me hard and drew blood for the first time in my entire life. He stood there, looking behind me with his hackles raised and hair standing on end. His teeth were bared but I noticed he still wasn't putting any weight on that back leg. I was angry he bit me but he looked so mean and vicious I didn't slap him like I wanted to. Now my hand was bleeding. I was afraid to turn and look behind me to see what my dog was growling at but since he wouldn't let me pick him up and I couldn't just leave him there, especially while he was injured, I felt like I had no choice but to turn around. I guess I thought that I would see some sort of animal or something but I never expected what I actually saw.

There, in the almost complete darkness of those woods, I saw creatures that terrify me still to this very day. There were three of them and they were all standing in a line between two trees and staring right at us. The only light I had was the light of the full moon but these beings or whatever they were seemed to have their own light source. I thought maybe that was the light I had seen from the house before my father had warned me not to go into the woods that night. They were dark blue and their eyes were glowing, golden yellow. They stunk to high heaven and I could see that they were wet. The water dripping from them looked black. I don't know how to explain it but I knew that it was the water from the swamp. They just stood there staring at me and my dog. The smell coming from them was like a mixture of rotting meat and feces. It was the most horrific thing I had ever smelled in my entire life. I couldn't take my eyes off of them and I couldn't run because I couldn't leave my injured, and very angry, dog behind. I didn't know what to do. I was only around eleven years old at the time and in my mind these beings or creatures were something straight out of one of the science fiction movies I loved so much. They were aliens! They didn't look like they were breathing but as I stood there thinking, my mind racing with every imaginable thought you could possibly think of, I noticed something. They weren't looking in my eyes or at my dog's eyes; they were looking at my hand and his back leg and paw. They were looking at the places on our bodies where we were injured and bleeding. They wanted our blood.

Suddenly one of them moved forward and my dog attacked. It all happened so fast it was almost like I simply blinked and it had my dog by the neck. The dog yelped and I was either going to run away or run at them and try to get my dog back. I screamed for them to let him go and they did. They threw him on the ground. He let out one final yelp and went limping, as fast as he could, off into the woods and towards home. I was afraid to take my eyes off of these terrifying creatures. Their mouths were now sneering at me and I knew they wanted my blood. When the one had my dog in the air it took a deep inhale of the dog's back leg. The injured and bleeding one. He sniffed it long and deep and then looked totally satisfied. That's when I yelled for it to release him. I knew these things would do worse to me and that I had to run home. Their teeth were sharp and the one who had grabbed my dog and advanced on me a few steps licked its lips. It had a forked tongue and everything. It was absolutely horrifying! I turned and ran as fast as I could. I finally stopped to take a breath, hoping and praying for all I was worth that they weren't following me. I had no idea if they were or not but I just couldn't run anymore. My poor dog came limping out to me from behind a tree right where I had stopped. I gently picked him up and told him it would be okay. I looked around and at first I saw nothing. I started walking back home.

I think by that point I was in a trance or in shock or something. I should have been running for my life and yet I couldn't put a single coherent thought together. I started giggling maniacally and my dog was struggling to get away from me. I wasn't letting him go and when I turned around I saw three balls of light hovering above a nearby rock. The lights were bright blue and at the time they looked beautiful to me. Something about them was drawing me in and I didn't realize I was approaching them. My dog tried to bite me again, probably in an effort to get away from me since I was now advancing on those balls of light which were, for sure, those creatures in a different form. Luckily my dog attacked me again, or tried to, because it probably saved both of our lives. I snapped back out of it immediately and turned to start running again. I was slowed down significantly by the weight of my dog in my arms. He was still scared and shaking, most likely still in pain, but he wasn't struggling against me anymore which made it easier. I made it home, went inside and called my neighbor who lived a few miles down the road. She was the emergency contact person I was supposed to call when my dad was at work and I was all alone. She came right away despite it being around six o'clock in the morning by that time.

I wasn't in the woods that long and I still have no idea what happened to the time. It's still completely missing from my memory. I wish dogs could talk because I believe he remembered every bit of it. He was never the same again but he was fine in the end and lived a long life. He was just less adventurous and didn't really ever want to leave the house after that night. Luckily the lady down the street believed everything I told her and said she would handle my father when he got home. She got me and the dog bandaged and cleaned up. She tucked me into bed just as the sun was rising and waited for my dad to get home. I don't know what she told him but he never asked me about it and I was forever grateful to her. I still explored the woods and swamp after that because I was hell bent on finding answers. I wasn't ever left alone again though because the lady down the street would always spend the night when my dad worked overnights and eventually, believe it or not, they married and she became my step-mother. It was awesome.

So anyway, that's my story. I'm sorry there isn't much more to it and I wish more than anyone I had more to report. I saw the strange blue lights in the woods many times since the night of the incident but she would never allow me to go out there and I noticed she wouldn't sleep on those nights either. I have had some nightmares throughout the years but I don't know if they mean anything. They are almost always an exact replay of what I remember from that night, from the time I chased my dog into the woods until I ran home and called the neighbor. I believe those creatures were extraterrestrials who possibly came to the area on the night of the storm

.I believe too that they live or feed off of animal and human blood and that's exactly what they were out to get that night. I don't know what they did to me or my dog during the missing time but the time had to have gone somewhere. I haven't seen many encounter stories about these same creatures but who knows, maybe someone out there has more answers for me.

———

Get the first volume in Ethan Hayes' new bestselling series
WHAT LURKS BEYOND, VOLUME I

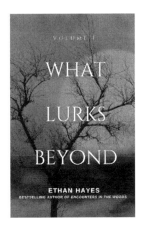

ALSO BY ETHAN HAYES

Encounters in the Woods, Vol. 1

Encounters in the Woods, Vol. 2

Encounters in the Woods, Vol. 3

Encounters in the Woods, Vol. 4

Encounters in the Woods, Vol. 5

Encounters in the Woods, Vol. 6

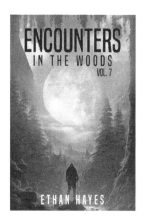

Encounters in the Woods, Vol. 7

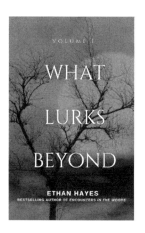

What Lurks Beyond, Vol. 1

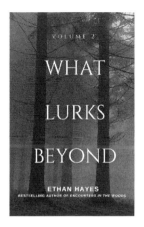

What Lurks Beyond, Vol. 2

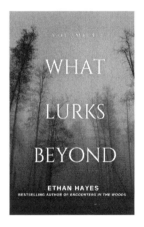

What Lurks Beyond, Vol. 3

ABOUT THE AUTHOR

Ethan Hayes grew up in Oklahoma and moved to Texas when he attended Texas A&M. Upon graduation he was hired by Texas Parks and Wildlife and remained there until he retired twenty-two years later. He currently lives in southeast Texas with his wife and two dogs. When he's not spending time enjoying the outdoors and writing, he sips a cold beer on his front porch while listening to Bluegrass music.

———

Send in your encounter story:
encountersbigfoot@gmail.com

Printed in Great Britain
by Amazon

21920268R00070